THE SEEDLESS TREES
A Fairy Tale

By Christina Waymreen

Dedication: To my cousin Andie, who mentioned once when we were children that if I ate too many grapes with seeds, vines would sprout from my nose and ears. I believed her.

Illustrated By John Nikolouzos (johnnikolouzos.daportfolio.com)

Library of Congress Catalog Number: 2014904988
BISAC: Fiction / Fairy Tales, Folklore, Mythology

ISBN-13: 978-0-9960132-0-8

Christina Waymreen

Contents

The Beautiful Trees

Once upon a time, when life was peaceful and full of joy, there was a small village quietly going about its business near the edge of a great forest. This tiny village was well known for its beautiful trees. There were tall trees and short trees, thick trees and thin ones; trees with leaves of every imaginary color and shape. Yet none of these trees flowered or bore fruit. Strangers, who asked in wonder, "How did they come to be?" would only get a shrug by the befuddled villagers themselves.

Each spring, King Dresdan and his son, Prince Lester, would pass by the village to witness the first new leaves, and each time they would sigh and say, "If only they bore seeds. One seed is all we need," and when the villagers shook their heads in regret they would continue on their way, a little bit sadder.

One spring day, when the first tiny leaves of the season unfurled, the King and his son rode by to admire the colors. This time the Prince's beautiful young bride, Anna, accompanied them. As they approached the village the young bride exclaimed. "Oh, my, what beautiful trees. I must have such trees in my garden. Oh, please, my dear husband, ask the villagers if they could sell me a tree, maybe a seed? One tiny seed is all I need."

When the Prince explained that it would be impossible as the trees bore no fruit or flowers and the villagers had no idea how the trees came to be, the Princess became deeply unhappy.

No amount of gifts could bring the smile back to her face. The Prince filled her garden with flowers and plants from different kingdoms but the Princess would only give him a slight nod of appreciation.

One day the Prince had an idea. "I will go to the village and uproot a tree. I will choose the smallest tree and replant it in our garden. I am sure that will bring the smile back to her face."

So the Prince, accompanied by his gardener, rode to the village to ask permission from the Governor if they could uproot one tree.

"It has only been done once, a very long time ago. I do not recall the details but I guess you can try," said the Governor. "I cannot guarantee that the tree will survive."

"Thank you, kind sir," replied Prince Lester. "I can only try."

The Prince with his gardener searched for the smallest tree and found it in the backyard of a small cottage. The Prince knocked on the door to ask permission from the owner. The door opened and a very old man, bent from the waist down, stared at his visitor. He could barely see or hear and did not recognize the Prince. In his hand he held a large, colorful horn woven from the fallen leaves of the beautiful trees. He put it to his ear.

"Eh, young man," he barked, "what is it you want?"

"I came to ask permission, sir, if I could uproot that small tree in your back yard for Princess Anna," said Prince Lester.

"What flea? I have no fleas."

"Not a flea, sir," said the Prince, raising his voice slightly. "A tree."

"Tree?" said the old man stepping up closer to the Prince to get a better look and still not recognizing him. "I have no trees. There are plenty over there," he said, waving his hand towards the majestic trees growing all along the side of the cobbled street.

"There is a tree in your backyard, sir," bellowed the Prince into the horn, "that I would like to uproot and plant in my garden for Princess Anna."

"You don't have to shout," cried the old man, turning his head away from the Prince. "That was my good ear. And where is this tree that you want to uproot, again?"

"In your backyard, sir," answered the Prince as patiently as he could.

"The last time I looked there was no tree," said the old man, scratching the side of his head. "I guess I will just have to look again. You never know with these trees. They just pop up anywhere with no warning."

They walked around the house and indeed there was a small tree with purple and gold leaves growing straight and proud right in the middle of the old man's backyard.

"You see," said Prince Lester pointing excitedly. "That one."

"Well, I don't know," said the elderly gentleman scratching his head again. "I am an old man and I have seen many things in my life. But what I do know is that no one has ever been able to remove one single tree from this village without dire consequences. Bad luck, you know," he added softly.

"Ha," cried Prince Lester, "tell me, sir, what is the nature of this bad luck?"

"Nothing that I can remember, at the moment," answered the old man, solemnly shaking his head. "I just know something bad happens. I am over a hundred years old I cannot remember everything."

"Well, it seems, since you cannot remember the nature of this bad luck it might not have been that bad at all. Now will you give us permission to uproot it?"

"Take it. One will eventually grow again," said the old man and shrugging his shoulders he shuffled back to his house.

The Prince and his gardener took out their shovels and began digging around the small tree. They dug deep into the ground until finally it was time to pull the tree out. As they pulled at the tree to dislodge it from its bed a loud, short shriek was heard. For a moment all the people in the village froze. The Prince and the gardener tumbled backwards as the tree let go of its hold in the ground. They looked around to find the source of the sudden frightening sound. Even the old man sitting in his little cottage snapped his head back. He suddenly remembered what he had forgotten. But it was already too late and he promptly forgot it again.

Christina Waymreen

Princess Anna

Prince Lester was delighted. He raced back to the palace and secretly planted the tree right next to their bedroom window. He could hardly wait to see the look on Princess Anna's face when she woke up the next day to see the beautiful tree with its purple and gold leaves, waving in the early morning breeze.

True to his wish Princess Anna was ecstatic. She clapped her hands and slipping on her red fuzzy slippers ran out the door in her nightgown early the next morning. She danced around the tree and kissed its leaves and ran her hands down its smooth trunk.

"Oh, this must be the most beautiful tree in the whole, wide world," she cried. "Thank you, thank you, thank you," she said to her husband, throwing herself into his arms.

The days passed by quickly. Each morning the Princess would wake up in the morning and stare out the window at her tree. Each morning she would kiss its leaves and fling her arms around its trunk and say, "You are the most beautiful tree in the world."

On the first day of spring, Princess Anna woke up early and ran to the window to see her cherished tree. The winter was exceptionally harsh and she had waited patiently for the first leaves to show. Amazingly, not only had the tree unfurled new purple and gold leaves, but had bloomed dazzling white flowers as well. Once again she raced outside in her red fuzzy slippers and nightgown. The air all around her was filled with a fragrance that would make a rose hide its head in shame.

"You are by far, without a doubt, the most beautiful tree in the world," she cried, hugging its thin trunk.

"You see," said the Princess, admonishing her husband, who was astonished to see the tree bloom, "all it needed was tender loving care."

A few days later a strong wind swept through the palace grounds, breaking branches and flinging everything it could from its path. As it roared around Princess Anna's tree all the flowers except one fell to the ground.

The Princess was disappointed but thankful that one blossom survived. Eventually that too dropped and a small, perfectly round, red fruit took its place.

"I wonder what this can be?" asked the Princess, one day, as she strolled through the garden with Prince Lester. She plucked the tiny fruit off

Christina Waymreen

its branch. "It smells good enough to eat. Maybe there is a seed inside and I can grow another tree just like this one," she said, turning to her husband.

"We can try," he said, smiling back at her. "But I don't know if one can eat it. I have never seen such fruit before. It could be harmful."

"Oh, no, my tree would never do that to me," she said, taking a tiny bite. "See? Delicious!"

"Well, that reminds me," said the Prince, laughing and rubbing his stomach. "It's dinner time. We can't keep the King waiting. We should be going back," he remarked, making a head start to the palace doors.

"Wait for me," cried Princess Anna.

The Princess took one step and stopped. Try as she might she could not pick up her foot and place it in front of the other. She looked back to see what was stopping her but there was nothing. It was as if her feet were stuck solidly to the ground. She screamed in alarm and looked up at her husband. As he ran back to her, he watched in horror as tiny branches shot out from her ears and mouth and quickly wrapped themselves around her body. It took only a few seconds and by the time the Prince managed to hold onto a branch wrapping itself around her waist she had disappeared and in her place a small tree with purple and gold leaves stood right next to the old one.

Prince Lester ran around the tree sobbing and wailing and tearing at his clothes until everybody in the palace ran outside to see what the commotion was all about. They would not believe what he was telling them until he pointed to the bottom of the tree. Sticking halfway out of the trunk, as if in mid-stride, were two red, fuzzy slippers.

The King embraced his son and wept loudly with him. It is nothing but evil witchcraft, he cried, and the villagers must be punished for this.

"I will chop every tree down and burn it, "The King said at the top of his voice. "I never want to see another tree as long as I live!"

But the Prince would not hear of it. He was afraid that more evil would manifest itself. There might be another way to rid themselves of those beguiling trees and bring his beloved back. The first thing he must do was to return to the village and get the old man to remember what it was he had forgotten.

Christina Waymreen

The Old Man

With a heavy heart Prince Lester knocked on the old man's door but there was no answer. He pounded angrily until his fist ached but still the old man did not reply. He raced around to the back. In the middle of the yard, two magnificent trees stood a few feet apart from each other. The trees were abundant with shiny, square leaves as bright as the sun and sprinkled with tiny black dots. A large hammock swung between the two trees and in it the old man lay fast asleep with his mouth wide open, emitting deep grunts and whistles.

"Wake up, old man," yelled the Prince, jabbing him in the shoulder. "Wake up!"

"What! What!" cried the old man, jolting awake. "Has the sky fallen?"

"My life has fallen apart," said the Prince, almost in tears. "You must help me!"

"Have I seen you before?" asked the old man, rubbing his eyes. "Your face looks familiar." He peered closely at the Prince.

"Yes, yes, you have," the Prince said loudly. "I was the one who uprooted your tree last year. You said there would be dire consequences and you were right. You must remember something to help me. You must help me," he cried, almost shaking the old man off the hammock.

The old man's eyes widened fearfully. "What dire consequences? What are you talking about?"

The Prince reminded the old man once again about his last visit and what had transpired after that.

The old man nodded his head. "Ah, yes, I remember now. Really? She turned into a tree?" He sighed deeply. "What bad luck."

"Yes, very bad luck," said the Prince, trying not to shake the old man again.

"You took the tree from my backyard, yes, I remember," he said, nodding his head.

"What about the bad luck? You said that it was done before and bad luck befell the person who took it," said Prince Lester.

"Did I say that? That, I don't remember," said the old man shaking his head sadly.

"Please remember," cried Prince Lester, grabbing the old man's gnarled fingers. "Please."

Christina Waymreen

"Sorry, I might have heard the story from the old lady in the village. She's a bit older than I am, you know. Maybe she still remembers something. Go ask her," he added, lying back on his hammock. "I hear she is on her death bed. Where does she live?" asked Prince Lester.

"Everybody knows where she lives. Ask anybody on the street and they will point the way to old lady Rose's place. That's her name. Old Lady Rose."

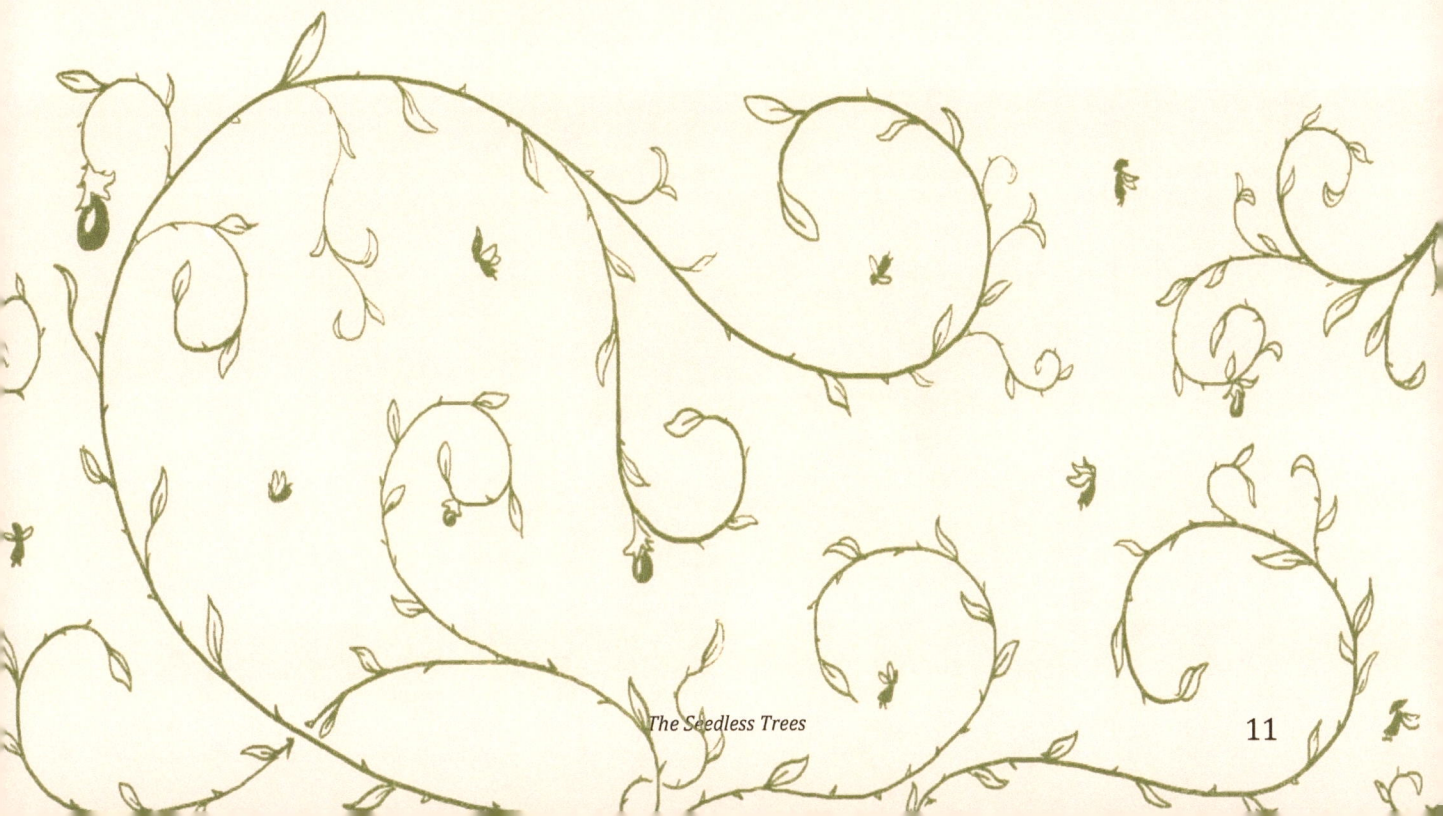

Old Lady Rose

The Prince ran back to the street and asked every man, woman and child he met which way to Old Lady Rose's house. Each one pointed him in the direction he had to take until he came upon a little girl with dark, curly hair.

"Which is the way to Old Lady Rose's house?" he asked her.

The young girl pointed to a cottage surrounded entirely by rose bushes at the corner of the street. "She lives there," she said, "but I haven't seen her in a long time. She usually sits on her porch."

The Prince thanked the young girl and sprinted up the stairs to the front door. He knocked loudly a few times and just when he had almost given up hope that she was still alive he heard someone fumbling at the latch.

"Who's there?" cried a voice.

"It's me, Prince Lester," he answered.

The door swung open and standing in front of him was a young woman with big, black eyes. "Your highness," cried the young woman, trying to curtsy and almost falling over.

"Does Old Lady Rose live here?" he asked unaware of the shock he gave her. "I need to speak to her. It is most urgent."

"She is ill, sire, dying."

"I must see her," said the Prince, pushing the girl aside, afraid the old lady would die any minute before he could reach her. He ran from room to room with the young woman following him until he came upon the bedroom. Inside a frail, wizened, woman lay in bed. Her thin white hair was spread all over a pillow and the Prince could feel that her final moment was near as her breathing was slow and raspy. He fell to his knees next to the bed and taking the old lady's hand he begged that she open her eyes one last time. The dying woman opened one beady eye and stared up at him.

"I am dying," she spoke slowly, almost whispering. "What is so important that you delay my passing?"

The Prince quickly explained what had taken place and beseeched the dying woman to help him.

"Ah, she has eaten the fruit of the seedless trees." She spoke softly. "I have heard of such a thing happening a very, very long time ago. Before my time, you know. Poor Rupert, he stands at the entrance of the village.

Nobody could help him. He moved a tree, too, you know. He ate of its fruit. You never eat the fruit."

"Yes, yes, I understand that now," Prince Lester said impatiently. "Do you know of anyone I could talk to that could help me? I beg of you."

The old lady opened her other eye and glared at the Prince. "When one is dying it is hard to remember all the conversations one has had in their life time."

Prince Lester's dark, brown eyes swelled with tears and slowly trickled down his cheeks, a few dropped on the old lady's withered face.

"You are desperate, I see." She slowly lifted her hand and patted him on the face.

"Let her die in peace, sire," said the young woman standing behind him. "She does not remember."

The Prince lowered his head onto the bed, his tears wetting the sheet.

"All I can tell you…" said Old Lady Rose wearily.

"Yes, yes," cried Prince Lester, jerking his head back up.

"Follow," she said, stopping for a moment and taking a small breath. "Follow the…"

The Prince squeezed the old lady's hand harder, which was by now as cold as an icicle.

"Follow…the…red…leaves."

"What red leaves?"

"The…red…leaves," she said and closed her eyes.

"You must go now," said the young woman, placing a gentle hand on the Prince's shoulder. "It is all that she can tell you."

The Prince reluctantly walked towards the bedroom door.

Christina Waymreen

"You know the way out," said the young woman. "I must stay here."

The Prince left the hut more desperate then ever. He could hardly look up and sadly walked back to where his horse was tethered. The news of Princess Anna's plight had spread rapidly throughout the village and everyone felt sorry for the young Prince and left him alone. A single red leaf fluttered to the ground and he picked it up, crushing it in his hand as a surge of anger overwhelmed him.

As he climbed onto his horse he looked up towards the forest. At the foot of the forest a tree, taller and thinner than all the trees in the village shimmered like the finest of rubies in the sunlight. "Follow the red leaves," he said to no one in particular. "Follow the red leaves." He opened the palm of his hand and stared at the crushed red leaf and looked again towards the thick forest. An identical red-leafed tree, a few meters behind the first one, poked its head above the rest of the forest, and another and another until the Prince finally understood.

"Now I know. I must follow the path these trees with the bright, red leaves make. I do not know what I will find. But it is a start."

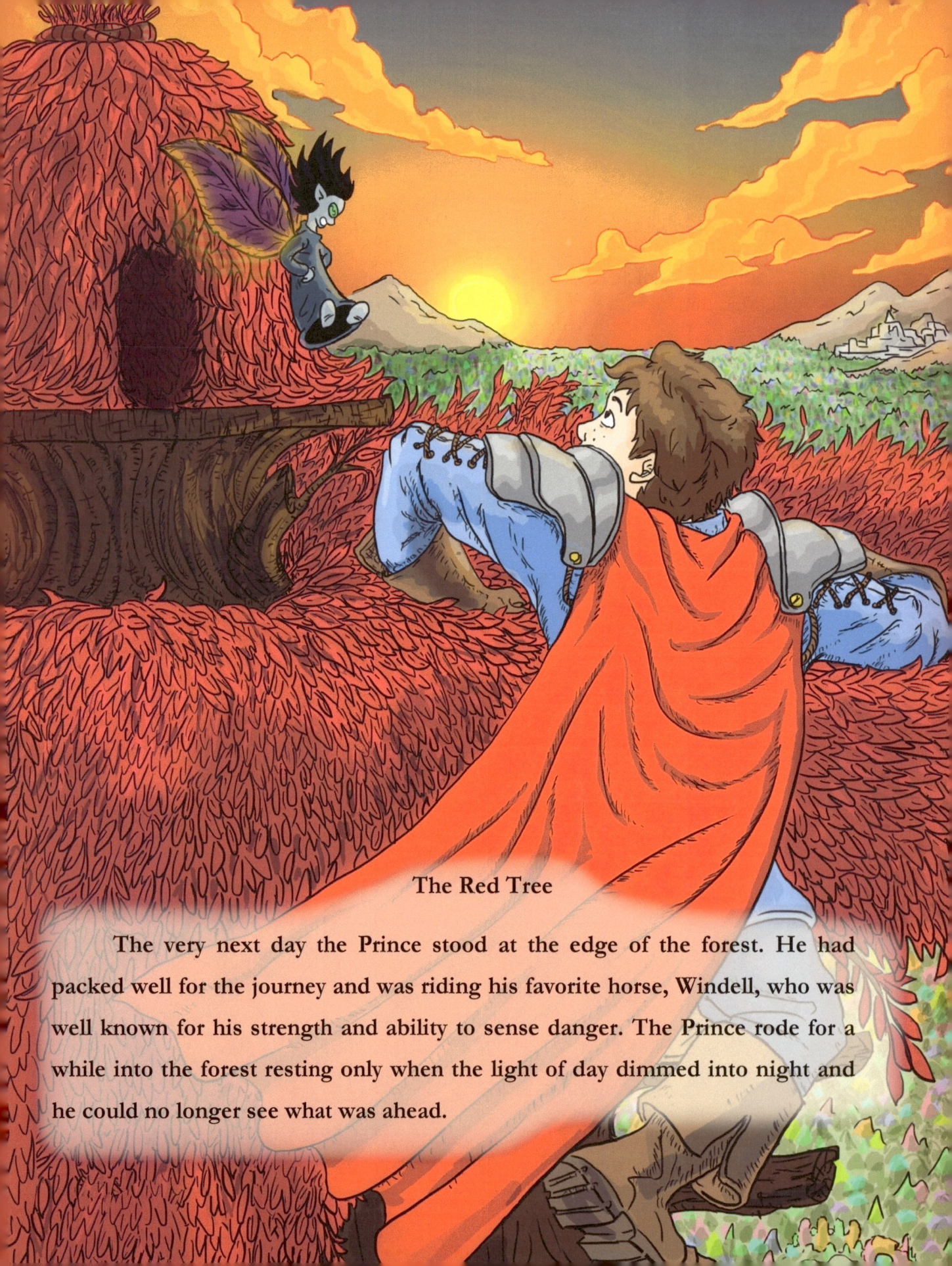

The Red Tree

The very next day the Prince stood at the edge of the forest. He had packed well for the journey and was riding his favorite horse, Windell, who was well known for his strength and ability to sense danger. The Prince rode for a while into the forest resting only when the light of day dimmed into night and he could no longer see what was ahead.

Finally, the next afternoon he was surprised to come upon a red tree like no other. Its trunk was so thick that it seemed almost impossible to see where it curved. It took the Prince a long while to ride around the large trunk and it was evening by the time he approached the back and came upon a wooden staircase that disappeared into the branches.

"This must be the end of the path," the Prince said as he dismounted from his horse.

Tying Windell to a leafy bush he took the stairs one by one, climbing higher and higher until he wondered if he was doing the right thing at all. On and on he climbed until he could hardly breathe and his legs grew weaker and weaker. When he thought that he could no longer move a muscle, he finally reached the end and collapsed onto a platform in front of a miniature hut that seemed to have been woven from the same ruby-red leaves. As he lay on his back panting, he wondered what kind of creature could live in such a small house.

When he felt a bit of his strength creeping back into his body he slowly stood up and gasped in amazement. He thought he was standing on top of the world. Below him the forest dazzled his eyes with color and light and the setting sun gave out a golden glow that enriched his senses, making his heart ache even more longingly for his beloved Anna. He could even make out the zigzag path he took through the forest, as the red trees were indeed taller than any other. Also, he noticed that he had reached the end of the forest and just a few miles to his left a wide raging river wound its way towards the mountains. Suddenly he heard a slight rustling behind him.

"You should not be here," somebody hissed at him.

The Prince turned as rapidly as his aching body would let him and was surprised to see a tiny, human-like creature floating above the open doorway of the hut. Instead of wings, two purple leaves were flapping on her back and the same type of leaf was wrapped around her body. With her big, green eyes she looked like a little bug.

"Who are you?" asked the Prince with a look of surprise.

"I am the Protector of the Forest!"

"One so small to protect a forest so large?" asked Prince Lester, his hand sweeping the air.

"We are many. Today I am in charge," she huffed.

"Then it is you who I must ask for help," said the Prince, hoping she had all the answers.

"In this forest we help no one."

"Oh, but you must," cried Prince Lester. "I have come a very long way. You see, my wife has turned into a tree and I must find a way to break the spell."

"It is what she deserves," she squeaked flying around him. "The moment you uprooted the tree from its sacred place we heard its shriek of agony. The Mistress of the Trees has punished you. Now be gone! Shoo!" she said, waving her hand at him as if he were nothing but a bug himself.

"This Mistress of the Trees," said Prince Lester as he headed towards the stairs, "where can I find her?"

"She is here, there and everywhere. She sees and hears all but is never seen and speaks to no one."

"But you must at least give me a hint. Something to start with."

"Shoo!"

The Prince sat down on the foot of the stairs and wearily lowered his head. He was very hungry and tired, and the thought of climbing down the stairs with no more information than what he came with, made him furious.

"You must tell me," he yelled, jumping up suddenly and trying to grab the flying creature that was now hovering above him. He almost had her by the feet but she quickly eluded him and flew into the small hut, slamming the door behind her. The Prince bent down and tapped on the door with his finger. "Go away! Shoo!" she screamed at him behind the safety of her door.

"Just tell me where she is and I will leave you alone."

Christina Waymreen

"No! Shoo!"

The Prince sat down on the stairs again to think. The sun had just dropped out of sight and he had no intention of climbing down the tree in the dark. He sat for a while until an idea formed in his head and then he curled up in the middle of the wooden deck and fell asleep.

Bug

Just as the sun threw its first rays into the early morning sky the Prince woke up and remembered his idea from the night before. He plucked a few leaves and taking out a knife from his pocket he cut them into thin, straight strips. Deftly he twisted and turned the strips until a few minutes later he had expertly woven a tiny, red basket with a lid.

Stepping over the small hut he bent down and waited patiently for the creature to come out. It was not too long before he heard the door open and out flew the human bug, stretching and yawning. Swiftly the Prince swooped her up in the makeshift cage and closed the lid.

"Now I have you," he said, smiling at her wickedly through the small spaces between the strips.

"You are a horrible man," she cried. "Free me immediately!"

"Not until you tell me where I can find the Mistress of the Trees."

"I told you yesterday. She is everywhere and speaks to no one," she yelled, trying to squeeze her body through the thin bars and failing as her leafy wings hindered her escape.

"That is not good enough. How can I get her attention?" asked Prince Lester, raising the cage closer to his face.

The little creature of the forest crossed her hands over her chest and huffed. "I know not."

"I think you do," he replied. "Somehow, I think you do and I will not free you until you tell me."

The prisoner only glowered at him. The Prince seeing he was getting nowhere at the moment with her decided it was time to climb down the tree. After all he had left Windell alone all night and he was beginning to be worried about him. It seemed to the Prince that it took hours to reach the bottom. On the way down he stopped for a moment and asked the creature's name but she refused to answer, turning her back on him, so he decided since she looked like a little bug he would call her that. When he finally took the last step he looked around for Windell but he was nowhere to be seen. The only thing he found was the leather pouch that he had removed from Windell's back and left on the ground.

"What have you done with my horse, Bug?" he shouted at her.

"I know nothing about your foolish horse," she replied, "and don't call me Bug."

"That is your name."

"No, it is not."

"Until you tell me what your real name is, Bug it will stay. Now where is my horse?" He asked angrily.

Before she could answer, he heard Windell's terrified neighing coming from behind some trees. Running towards the sound he came upon a clearing and stopped in shock. Windell was in the center of a circle of creatures much the same as his captive. His eyes were rolling in fear and his head snapped back and forth trying to free himself from their tight grasp on his reins. Next to the horse a huge pit had been dug and a blazing fire bellowed from its depth.

"Free her," the creatures cried, "or your horse shall die."

The Prince stood stunned for a moment not knowing what to do. "I only wanted information."

"We have none to give," said one of the creatures, whose wings were made from the very tree that he had grown to hate. On seeing the gold and purple wings, Prince Lester's face grew ugly and mean.

"No," he said, and jumping through the circle, he ran towards the fiery pit, raising the box with the captive Bug as near as possible to the flames without hurting her. "My horse dies, Bug dies."

For a moment it seemed that the forest fell silent. The tiny creatures flitted around not knowing what to do, frantic that their plan had backfired.

"Wait," cried the creature with the gold and purple wings that seemed to be the leader of the small group, "do not be hasty. What kind of information are you looking for?"

"Tell me where I can find the Mistress of the Trees," he demanded.

"Such information only leads to death," said the leader.

"Whose death?" asked Prince Lester.

"Yours," Bug hesitated for a moment, "and ours."

"I do not believe you," said Prince Lester

"You must. We have pledged to her on pain of death never to reveal her whereabouts."

"Then there must be someone who has no allegiance with her. Someone who has not pledged their life to her," said the Prince, stepping slightly away from the fire.

"I think there is," said another of the forest creatures wrapped in blue leaves. "Only a few miles away from here the forest clears and you will come upon a river. Follow the river up hill. You will then come to a waterfall. Behind the waterfall lives a beast. It will tell you where the Mistress of the Trees resides."

"Why should I believe you?"

"Because we are the Protectors of the Forest. We tell no lies."

The Prince stood silent for a while, thinking. After a few moments he stepped towards the flames and raised the box.

"Please," they cried again in unison, "we tell no lies!"

"Then let go of my horse and step away."

They let go of the reins and flying up towards the nearest branches, sat down. The Prince flung his leather pouch on Windell's back and climbed into the saddle.

"Do not follow us," he said, looking up. "Once I reach the edge of the forest I will let Bug free."

"My name is not Bug!" shrieked the prisoner, shaking the bars of her cage. "It's Gladiola!

"Huh, at last," said Prince Lester mustering a short laugh, "but I still prefer Bug."

Once the Prince rode out of the forest he opened the box. Gladiola flew out adjusting her leaves.

"Were you really going to throw me into the fire?" she asked pouting.

"No, I have never in my life been cruel to anyone," he said. "Not even a bug. Were you going to throw my horse into the fire?"

"Yes," said Gladiola and quickly flew back to the protection of the trees.

24   *Christina Waymreen*

The River Master

The Prince rode on, somewhat wary if they had told him the truth or not. He had forgotten to ask what kind of beast it was that lived behind the waterfall but he had no alternative now but to go on. After a few hours he decided to stop and rest. The river was teaming with fish and after building a fire he easily caught his supper.

As he placed the fish on the hot stones, Windell suddenly grew restless and started to neigh and buck. Prince Lester searched around to find the cause of his horse's distress but could not see anything. After calming the horse, he sat down to eat his supper.

"I do not remember giving you permission to fish in my waters," a voice boomed from the river.

Prince Lester dropped the remaining piece of fish he was eating and jumped up. The river had stopped flowing and a limpid face appeared in its depth. Then, like a tidal wave, a watery body rose up, sucking the river dry. The head almost touched the skies and he could still see the fish swimming within its liquid frame.

Prince Lester backed away, ready to jump on Windell and run like the wind, but a huge watery hand picked him up and dangled him in the air.

"Who gave you permission to fish in my waters?" the enraged water giant bellowed in his face.

"Who are you?" screamed Prince Lester, kicking his feet in the air. "I was hungry. I meant no harm."

"I am the River Master. You have not asked my permission."

"Then, please, accept my apologies. How can I pay you for my misdeed?" Asked Prince Lester as fear gripped at his heart, making it race wildly.

"Your apology, accepted. Your payment, death by drowning." Without warning the River Master flung his head back, and tossing the Prince into his gaping mouth, snapped it shut.

The Prince took a deep breath before he plunged feet first into the water. All around him fish swam oblivious to his plight. He tried to push his way out but the water giant's frame only stretched like rubber and he could not break through. Knowing that he could not hold his breath any longer, the Prince took out his knife and stabbed at the rubbery walls. Suddenly the River Master changed his form again and flowed back into the dry riverbed.

Christina Waymreen

Feeling the change, Prince Lester kicked as hard as he could and swam upwards breaking the surface of the water. He took a deep breath but it was not over yet. The river grew fiercer and Prince Lester found himself swept up by a raging current that sent him upstream so fast it was all he could do to keep his head above water.

Onwards the river carried him, banging him into rocks and submerging him for long moments until the Prince felt that he could no longer manage to keep himself alive. His final wrenching thought, before he blacked out, was that he had failed to save his beloved Anna.

The Beast

A spray of mist hit his face again and again waking the Prince up from his stupor. The bottom half of his body was floating in a small pond and the other half lay on a hard rock just on its banks. He could hear water thundering from a distance. Something poked him repeatedly in the side and he looked up to see what it was. A thin branch, twisted and disfigured, poked him again.

"Are you alive?" it asked. "Have you come to save me?"

"Who are you?" croaked the Prince in astonishment, raising himself slightly.

A tree, no taller than five feet, stood above him, dry and cracked and totally leafless. Only two branches stuck out from the sides of its trunk and withered roots gathered at the bottom. What seemed like a mouth and two large, pleading eyes stared back at him from the center of the trunk.

Prince Lester tried to stand up but he felt giddy, and sat quickly down on the nearest rock.

"Who are you?" he asked again, wiping the mist off his face. The sight of the ungainly tree shocked him.

"I am Tara. Sometimes they call me The Beast. But I am no beast. I am only a poor, lonely woman who has failed in her mission."

"Oh," he said, not knowing what else to say.

She slithered towards him. "Have you come on the same mission?" she asked. "Have you come to save a loved one?"

"Yes, my wife," said Prince Lester. "And you?"

"My husband, Rupert."

"Ah, Rupert. I have heard of him," said the Prince. "Is he the one who stands at the entrance of the village of those evil trees?"

"The very tree," she said, sighing. "He would not listen to me, alas. He ate of the fruit."

"How did you fail? Is it something I can overcome?"

"Yes, maybe, I do not know," said Tara. From her eyes, large drops of sap oozed and flowed down the trunk. "Forgive me. I am a sorry sight."

"What happened to you?" asked Prince Lester, softly.

"I was hungry," she said, moaning. "I was hungry."

Tara continued to explain how she crossed through the forest, fought off the River Master and finally when she came to the waterfall she rested behind its safe walls. When she woke up she went in search for food knowing that she could not touch the fish in the river with or without permission. After a long search, she found a mushroom growing between thick green cloves in the dark shades of the forest. She tore it from the ground and raced back to the cave behind the waterfall. As she took a bite she felt her body twist and thrash. The Mistress of the Trees' ugly spells had transformed all the goodness in the forest to evil. Somehow the protection of the cave stopped her from becoming a complete tree. Many years passed and she had given up hope that anyone would ever come and rescue her.

"You mean I can eat nothing?" asked Prince Lester, feeling his stomach begin to churn.

"Nothing," she replied.

"Where can I find this Mistress of the Trees? How can I get rid of her once and for all?" he growled. Hunger pangs gripped him again, making him irate.

"In the morning, between dawn and dusk a black rainbow appears in the sky. I see it often. Every morning I wake up to glimpse it. For that is all you get. A glimpse and then it is gone. The rainbow starts from the very edge of the waterfall and curves along the sky. At the end of this rainbow lives the Mistress of the Trees. You must ride the rainbow. And remember, eat nothing."

"How can I ride a rainbow? It's impossible!"

"If you can seize it just as it appears it will recede back to its origin taking you along," she said.

"And do you know how I can rid the world of this Mistress of Darkness, for that she is," he said bitterly.

"You must find out what she fears the most."

"Have you found out?"

Christina Waymreen

"I failed as you can see," she said, as more gray sap flowed down her dried trunk.

"And if I am able to succeed will everything turn back to normal?" asked Prince Lester

"Yes," she said, sighing deeply as more tree sap dripped to the ground. "As if nothing ever happened."

The Black Rainbow

Morning broke and the Prince stood waiting and ready for the black rainbow to appear. It came suddenly and vanished just as quickly before he could grasp onto it. It frustrated him no end and the need for food increased with every hour. Shortly before the day came to a close, Windell entered the cave and the Prince's relief on seeing him was immense.

He ate what was left in his bag, offering Tara the same. But she could not eat of it. Tara promised to take care of Windell while he was gone.

"If only I can take a hold of the rainbow before I starve to death." Prince Lester moaned.

The next day, Prince Lester, hungry again and with the final morsel of food spent, stood right at the spot he had marked where the rainbow appeared the day before. As the sun peaked over the horizon, he grabbed onto the black strip just as it shot across the sky and landed at his feet. This time he quickly clamped onto the unsightly rainbow and as it receded he was flown with tremendous speed across the sky. He dared not look down and before he could take a second breath the rainbow disappeared and he dropped and tumbled along a rocky slope, landing painfully on his back. Opening his eyes he looked straight up and gasped. Hundreds of rainbows stretched across the sky in all their brilliance. He wondered where they all led but he had more important things to do than to imagine what lay at the end of those heavenly rainbows. He had to find the Mistress of the Trees before he succumbed to starvation and failed his beloved Anna.

At the top of a hill stood one large ominous looking tree with its branches spread wide and deep. Its leaves were shaped like stars and were of a deep ruby red much like the color of the trees that led him to the Protectors of the Forest. A golden door and two golden windows framed the tree trunk. Other than the rainbows and the gigantic tree there was nothing else on the lonely terrain.

Prince Lester staggered up the hill and he gasped for breath at every step. As he neared the golden door he smelled something delicious. He could feel his stomach gurgling and protesting loudly. Picking up a stone that fit nicely in the palm of his hand, he hurled it at the door.

"Who knocks at my door with such insolence!" He heard an angry voice cry from within the gigantic tree.

"It is I, Prince Lester," he shouted. "Come out and face me, oh Mistress of the Trees, if that is your name."

A face appeared at a window framed in gold and so hideous that the Prince covered his face from the sight of it.

"Oh, what ugliness is this," he cried.

"Not only are you insolent but extremely rude as well," she hollered from behind a glass window.

Realizing that he had spoken his thoughts out loud the Prince lowered his hands and squinted." Forgive me," he said. "What I meant is that… all around is…. hideous compared to your beauty."

"Well, that's more like it, come on in then. I am sure you must be hungry. I live at the end of nowhere. It must have been a long journey for you."

The door flew open and the Mistress of the Trees stood in all her glory. She was shaped like a tree trunk and thin branches with clear-blue leaves slithered from holes all around her body like writhing snakes. Prickly thorns protruded from the top of her head. Spattered across her cheeks and forehead were tiny wart-like bumps. Instead of a nose a snout protruded from the middle of her face.

"Come in. Come in," she said. "You're not bad looking yourself."

Prince Lester shuddered and walked slowly towards the door, his eyes watering as he neared her. She stepped aside to let him through and slammed the heavy gold door behind him.

"It has been a long while since I have had any visitors," she remarked. "Make yourself comfortable while I bring you something to eat. I have roast mutton covered in delicious gravy with baby carrots. A regular feast."

Inside he was amazed at the opulence and luxury she was living in. The chairs and sofas were covered in silk and paintings of birds and nature adorned her walls.

She came in carrying a tray filled with food and a jug of wine and placing it on a table ordered him to eat. Prince Lester was famished and picked up a fork. As he dug into the mutton and raised the juicy bit to his mouth he heard a voice in his head. "Remember, eat nothing." He dropped the fork and sat back.

"I'm not hungry at the moment," he said, his voice and hand trembling.

"You must be," she said with a slight snarl. "Everybody is hungry who comes to my door."

"Well, not me. I ate before I came."

"Here," she said, picking up his fork and digging once again into the mutton. "One little, teensy, weensy bite."

"No," yelled Prince Lester, backing away from her. "I told you. I'm not hungry."

"I said eat!" she snapped at him, her snout quivering.

"No!" he cried.

"I can play this game better than you can. Let's see how long you can stay without food, my handsome prince," she yelled and grabbing him by the scruff of his neck dragged him towards a door. The Prince kicked out but she was taller and stronger and managed to hold him with only one hand while opening the door with the other. She threw him into a bare room.

"When you are hungry just call me," she said, throwing her head back and screeching. "Just call me!"

Mistress of The Trees

The Prince looked around. The room was small and circular and somewhat damp. A window, heavily barred, curved to one side. He sat against the wall and closed his eyes. Had he failed just like Tara?

A loud knocking at the door woke him up. Outside, the patter of rain beat against a small window. He had been dreaming that he was standing in a field with his father. They were practicing sword fighting and it had begun to rain very hard. He wanted to continue but his father said it was too dangerous to fight in a storm, something about lightning and swords. He could not recall very well. The next thing he remembered about the dream was that he was sitting at the dinner table with his beloved Anna enjoying a fine meal. As his eyes fluttered open he heard The Mistress of the Trees bark at him from behind the door.

"Are you hungry yet?"

"No," he answered in a weak voice.

"I can't hear you!" she shouted.

"I said no!"

"You will be soon," she said. He could hear her voice cackling like dried burning logs.

The Prince rested his head against the wall. Find her fear, he thought, I must find what she fears the most. He thought and thought for a long time while staring out the window until his head ached and he could no longer bear the emptiness of his stomach. By then the sky had darkened even more and the rain pounded harder against the tree trunk. Suddenly a bolt of lightning cracked through the sky and smashed into the ground, almost hitting the tree. He heard a scream of terror.

"Oh, save me, save me!" The Mistress of The Trees wailed.

The Prince walked up to the door and banged hard. "I cannot save you if I am behind closed doors."

Suddenly the door flung open with such force that the Prince almost fell back into the room.

"Are you ready to eat now?" she asked as if nothing had happened.

He could tell from the way the gruesome branches on her body were frantically writhing and the way her hands were clenched that she was extremely agitated.

"No, somehow, I have lost my appetite, thank you," he said.

"Well, then why don't you have some des…" before she could finish another bolt of lightning cracked across the sky, sending the Mistress of the Trees screeching in alarm and frantically trying to find somewhere to hide. She threw herself under a table.

"So," he said, bending down to look at her, "scared of lightning?"

"Don't be silly," she said, waving a branch at him. "I think I lost something. It must be under here somewhere. Why don't you join me?" she asked, reaching out to grab his hand.

The Prince deftly avoided her grasp. "Why don't I just take a look outside?"

Suddenly an earsplitting sound pierced the room and the tree groaned. Something snapped and hit the ground. The Prince jumped in fear. He ran towards the front door but it was locked. The dream came back to him again and he remembered what his father said about playing in a storm with his sword. It is dangerous, my son, he could hear him say, dangerous.

If I can only get outside, thought Prince Lester, I might find a way out of this. "Where is the key to the door?" asked Prince Lester angrily.

"Here it is, my handsome Prince," the Mistress of the Trees cried. She stood behind him, dangling the large golden key in her hand. "The storm will pass, dearie, it always does."

The Prince jumped towards her but she was faster and skipped out of his reach.

"We shall brave the storm together. Why don't we sit and have some supper until it passes?" Her wooden lips trembled and her eyes darted to the window as lightening lit up the sky.

"Never, you hideous beast," he yelled above the raging storm. "I have come to save Anna and save her I will!"

The Mistress of the Trees' face grew darker and her voice took on a tone more menacing and terrifying than the tempest roaring outside.

"You will never leave this place alive. If you will not eat then I will kill you with my bare hands, you impudent man. I have tolerated you enough." She advanced towards him, the thin, wiry branches from her body stretched out to grab him. A loud cracking sound burst through the room, sending her scuttling again to the safety of the table. She dropped the key as she shoved her massive trunk under it.

The prince grabbed the key and ran back to the door. He pushed the golden key into the lock and turned it twice. The door opened with ease and as he stepped out, a bolt of lightning smashed into the ground. He could smell burning wood. Without a second thought he grabbed a low branch and pulled himself up into the tree. Hurriedly he climbed his way to the top from limb to limb.

Pulling his sword out of its sheath, he tied it with his leather belt against the tip of the highest branch. Quickly he descended and as he was half way down he felt a lightening bolt hit the tree with a mighty force, its sound almost piercing his eardrums.

Prince Lester climbed down as fast as he could. Barely reaching the bottom, he threw himself off the tree as it split in two.

The Mistress of the Trees stood furious between the ruined remains of her home, the rain still pouring down in sheets. "You have destroyed my home," she screamed in anger. "You think you are clever. You think I am afraid of the storm!"

"Yes" he snapped back, "It is lightning you fear the most. What else can destroy a tree with one blow?"

"You are a fool to speak so bravely only seconds before your death." She advanced towards him.

"It is your death you should be fearful about!" The prince cried. He stepped back and stumbled on a thick root protruding from the ground.

The Mistress of the Trees moved slowly towards him. Thin wiry branches shot out from the tiny openings in her massive body and wrapped themselves tightly around the Prince.

"Now, I have you, my Prince," Her cruel laughter smothered by the pouring rain. "Do you have any last words?"

The prince struggled but could not unwrap himself from the binds that held him. He looked around to see if there was anything that he could find to cut the vines. As he looked up in frustration a thick bolt of lightening, streaked through the dark clouds, breaking the sky in half, and headed straight towards them. The impact sent him flying a good distance away.

Goodbye," said the prince as he watched the Mistress of the Trees explode into flames. "You are really nothing but an ugly tree."

Christina Waymreen

Going Home

Finally, everything came to an end. The smoky charred remains of the giant tree lay in two heaps on top of the hill and the dark clouds parted, allowing the sun to shine in all its brilliance on the empty landscape. A perfect rainbow appeared, flinging itself across the sky as if in gratitude, and landed right at the Prince's feet.

He grabbed the end of the rainbow and was lifted up gently, sailing over the ground, finally coming to the bank of the river next to the waterfall.

Windell was standing nearby and on his back sat a beautiful woman, her smile so wide it almost split her face in half.

"Welcome home," said Tara.

They were both eager to return to the village. Prince Lester grabbed a hold of Windell's reins and they started along the bank of the river. After a short while an old man in white robes stepped out from behind some rocks. He bowed before Prince Lester.

"You may fish in the river anytime, Sire."

"And who are you?" asked the prince.

"I was once an old man who found himself bound by the Mistress of the Trees to protect the waters from anyone wishing to use them. I was the River Master but now no longer. I have you to thank, Sire."

Prince Lester thanked the old man and soon he and Tara were enjoying a meal along the rocky bank.

"It is good to eat real food after such a long time," said Tara as she took a bite from the fish that the Prince had cooked for them.

Soon they reached the edge of the forest. The trail of the red trees had disappeared and in its place was an empty, beaten path.

As they reached the middle of the road a young woman stepped out from behind a tree. She was as tall as the prince and was dressed in a light green dress that reached down to her bare feet. Windell reared in fear almost dropping Tara to the ground.

"Who are you that has such an effect on Windell?" asked Prince Lester to the woman.

"I am…" the young woman hesitated. "I am Gladiola."

"Ah, Bug, it is you," exclaimed Prince Lester. "You have changed."

Christina Waymreen

Gladiola blushed. "Yes, Sire, and it is all thanks to you. Our people lived peacefully in the forest until the Mistress of the Trees transformed us into the Protectors of the Forest. We owe our freedom to you."

Prince Lester said he was glad to have been of help and continued on his way. The trip back home was shorter and soon the forest gave way and they stood on the edge looking down on the village. The infamous trees had disappeared and only the beauty of nature spread its colors around the small town.

"What a beautiful sight to behold," cried Tara.

"Yes, said Prince Lester. "As it should be."

Tara let out a scream of delight. "Rupert," she cried as she spied her husband standing near the village gates. She jumped off Windell's back and ran happily towards him.

Prince Lester leaped into the empty saddle and ran Windell hard towards the castle. Waiting for him in the garden, with her arms outstretched, was his beloved Anna.

The End

About the Author

Christina was born in Detroit, Michigan. She finished high school in Jerusalem (West Bank) called the Schmidt's Girls College. Why they called a school a college is still a mystery to her. After graduating from the "college" she made her way to Kharkov, Ukraine where she found herself taking computer science and civil engineering, which she still knows zilch about. She spent her free time between classes wandering through bookstores, marveling at the Russian books so beautifully illustrated, especially those that were written for children. After a life in the travel industry, where she had the opportunity of visiting many places, some she doesn't remember, she finds herself, once again, in the country of her birth, soaking up the Florida sun and finally finding the time to start her next chapter in life with writing. She hopes it works out. You can contact the author at seawaypress@gmail.com.